For my beep bops: Noah, Milo, Zen and Lotus
and for my sister Nefeterius who loved hip hop

www.theenglishschoolhouse.com

ISBN: 978-1-955130-11-0

DJ THE KID DJ

BOOM
BOOM
POW!

BOOM
BOOM
POW!

KIDDI-BOOM

By Dr. Tamara Pizzoli - Illustrated by Adam Cox

Damilola Jaiyeola Oni, or D. J., as her family and friends called her for short, had been a music lover for as long as she or anyone she knew could remember. Jazz, salsa, merengue, the blues, classical—D.J. loved it all, but what she adored most of all was hip hop.

EATNIKS HEPCATS

MARTHA & THE VANDELLAS
COME AND GET THESE MEMORIES

BIG UP

HIPHOP TIL · YOU DROP

D.J. THE KID DJ
DJ

While parents of other children swooned when their kids babbled "goo goo" and "gaga", D.J. stunned her mom and dad when she rapped for the first time.

Even though my milk is tasty and great, I want to eat chicken nuggets from your plate!

STRAIGHT OUTTA KINDERGARTEN

MO' PACI MO' PROBLEMS

I guess she's ready for solids!

Get Harvard on the phone, honey! She's a genius!

Dr. Dre's guide to childcare

D.J.'s musical musings made sense. The entire Oni family had the gift of rhythm and song. During holidays and special occasions, they'd meet at D.J.'s great-grandmother Lillian's home for feasts and fellowship and music.

There was D. J.'s mom on the piano keys, her dad on drums, Uncle Sebastian on bass, Aunt Rose on trumpet, cousin Madya on the kora, and great-grandpa Benjamin blowing the saxophone, all while her great-grandmother Lillian sang her favorite tunes from the past.

D.J. liked to contribute a little something modern to the vibe.

Poom poom pow!
Poom poom pow!
My name's D.J.
I move the room like wow!

Oh Lord, I can't understand that racket...

But Granny, hip hop is just poetry set to music!

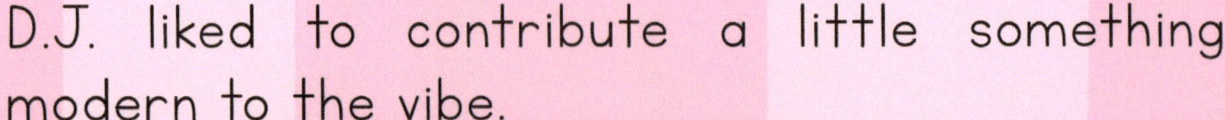

The only thing the family enjoyed more than making music together was sitting together to watch the hit television show *So You Want to Be a Star.*

Well, almost everyone was seated...

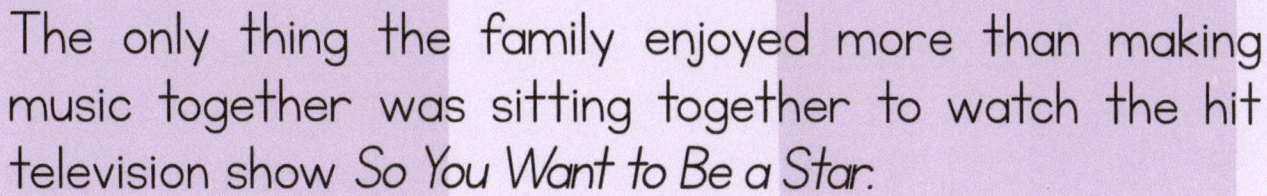

So You Want to be A STAR

Granny *please* have a seat. I can't see!

At school, D.J. kept her rhymes fresh by practicing every chance she got. She'd rap the lunch menu for her friends in the cafeteria.

Alright you guys check it.
I'll say this once and don't you forget it.

On the menu today they've got Brussels sprouts, corn, and baked chicken or that may be trout.

To drink they're giving us milk or juice
And then for dessert, we'll snack on some fruit.

9.5

EAT YOUR GREENS!

9

LUNCH

Everyone's a critic!

Apple

10

7

SUPER SQUAD

DJ appreciated the feedback.

One day D.J.'s family was in Grandma Lillian's living room, waiting for *So You Want to Be a Star* to begin.

Just as D.J. was about to run to the kitchen for a snack, her grandmother grabbed her hand and shrieked, "D.J.! This is for you!" There it was written on the screen: Auditions now open!

A week later D.J. was among an endless stretch of all sorts of performers waiting to audition. There were singers, breakdancers, a professional crier, flame throwers, comedians, interpretive dance troupes, a gospel choir, a bird whisperer, polyglots, poets, jugglers and at least one ventriloquist.

When her number was called, D.J. wheeled her equipment into the room where the three judges were seated. D.J. cleared her throat and softly said, "I'm Damilola. Everyone calls me D.J. I'm a rapper."

JUDGES

So You Want to be A STAR

But when D.J. pressed play to start her prerecorded music, her nerves got the best of her. She couldn't get a word out.

She ran out of the room and straight into the arms of her parents and grandmother.

"Done so fast?" her father beamed.

"No!" D.J. mumbled nervously, "I can't do it. I'm too nervous. I'm not ready."

"Nonsense!" her grandmother grinned. "You march right back into that room, take a deep breath, and use your gift! Let the words come to you!"

AUDITIONS THIS WAY!

QUIET PLEASE

So You Want to be A STAR

And if you get nervous, just imagine everybody in the room in their underwear...

...riding a dinosaur!

STAGE 4

D.J. reentered the judges' room.
Her grandmother's advice worked like a charm,
and D.J. was unanimously voted to the next round.

Did she just tell us what to do?

When I was in here before, I just ran away.
But I hurried right back with my mic to say,
I'm the kid DJ and I belong on this show!
So put me in the next round!
Show me where to go!

BOOM
BOOM
POW!

BOOM
BOOM
POW!

D.J. was among a total of nine performers selected by the judges to advance to the second round. In this round, each audience member held a special voting remote that allowed them to select their favorite performers.

So You Want to be A

STAR

VOTE FOR YOUR FAVORITE

So You Want to be A STAR

RAP IS POETRY

GO D.J.!

YOU CAN DO IT!

Y'ALL BETTER VOTE FOR MY GRANDBABY!

D.J. was impressed by the range of talent.
There were so many incredible and mesmerizing acts...

...and a few unconventional ones.

Tonight on
So You Want to Be a Star-
Who's Advancing to Round 3?
Will it be...

Jamal and his interpretive dance

Bob the Barking Human
and His Canine Companion

Sasha and Samuel, the Salsa Duo

Belen the Bird Whispering Ballerina

Noe the Mind Reader

Pietro the Speedy Portrait Maker

... Or D.J. the Kid DJ?

D.J. felt confident about her performance. She rapped words that came straight from her heart.

Brian Seacrest began, "Nine of you stand before me. As you know, only three can advance to the final round."

The tension in the air was palpable.
"When I call your name, please step forward."

"Belen... Jamal... Noe the Mind Reader... You're IN! The rest of you guys are unfortunately out. Don't forget to leave your number tags before leaving the building—we recycle those."

D.J. was completely stunned. Her name had not been called.

D.J., and the other eliminated contestants began exiting stage left, as she tried with all her might to stall the tears that were threatening to fall.

Just as she was about to pass the backstage curtain, one of the judge's voices rang out...

"Hold up!" his words boomed. "I'm gonna do something that's rarely ever done on this show. I'm using my special pass to save D.J. the Kid DJ this round. For the final competition there will be four contestants, but only one can win!"

That evening D.J.'s entire family gathered at her grandmother's home.

Those judges would have had to deal with me if they hadn't kept my grandbaby in that competition!

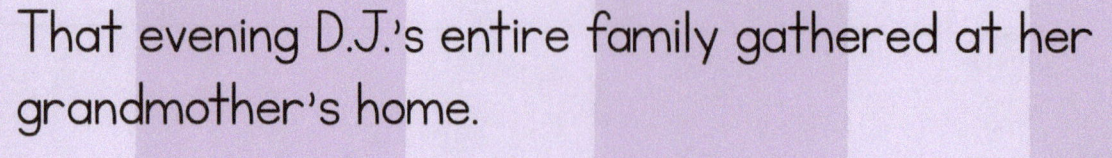

Granny, please!

"I'm up against two dancers and a psychic, and they're all grown up so they've been doing this a long longer than I have! How do I compete with that?"

The room fell quiet. After a few moments, Grandma Lillian spoke:

"People love to have a good time, D.J. Seems to me that the important thing isn't how long you've been doing what you do, but how well you do it. And no one raps as well as you do!"

Granny *knows* Best

D.J. awoke feeling prepared and focused when the final day of the competition arrived. She'd practiced her rhymes for days, her music was cued up and ready, and she'd tried out her rhymes on everyone she knew.

Brian Seacrest reintroduced the four finalists in his opening monologue. D.J. tried to stay focused on the words she'd prepared.

So, Noe, any ideas of who might win the competition tonight?

As far as I can see, I am the winner!

The contestants started their performances:

Noe the Psychic wowed the audience with his knowing and intuition.

Belen moved and grooved her way into viewers' hearts yet again.

CHIRP

TWEET TWEET

HONK! HONK!

DANCE FEVER

Jamal stunned the crowd with his powerful interpretive dance.

But it was D.J. and her riveting raps, set to an irresistible beat, that had the crowd and judges on their feet, swaying and shaking and stomping and shouting, and it was D.J. who stole the show.

So You Want to be A STAR

So You Want to be A **STAR**

D.J. the Kid DJ WINS

MY GRANDBABY IS A STAR!! ★